My Dad!

Written by
Chae Strathie

Illustrated by
Jacqueline East

meadowside
CHILDREN'S BOOKS

My dad tells me tales
of incredible things,

Like how he once sprouted
a great pair of wings.

He's been to the end
of the rainbow I'm told.
And guess what he found there?

A pot full of gold!

He says that one night
he flew to the moon,

By holding on tight
to a bunch of balloons.

While sailing at sea
on a stripy giraffe,
He says he saw
sea monsters…

...taking a bath!

He lived on the beach
in a house made of sand,

And played the guitar
in a maritime band.

He took on a
dragon that
lived in
a cave,

And rescued the princess
– how terribly brave!

He built
his own robot
with springs
in its feet,

Then sat on its shoulders
and bounced down the street!

He says that he worked
as a top-secret spy,

You'd never have known
he was hiding nearby.

He drove 'round
the world in a
motorized
bed,

And balanced a hippo
on top of his head.

But if I cry out,

"Please stop telling these tales
of talking tomatoes and
tap dancing whales!"

He always says one thing
I know to be true,
When he gives me a cuddle and says…

"I love you!"

For Reuben
J.E.

With love to beautiful Corinna Venus
and my bonnie wee Eilidh
C.S.

First published
in 2007 by
Meadowside Children's Books

185 Fleet Street, London,
EC4A 2HS

Text © Chae Strathie 2007
Illustrations ©
Jacqueline East 2007

The rights of Chae Strathie and
Jacqueline East to be identified
as the author and
illustrator of this work
have been asserted by
them in accordance
with the Copyright,
Designs and Patents
Act, 1988

A CIP catalogue record for
this book is available from
the British Library

Printed in China

10 9 8 7 6 5 4 3 2 1